To Sam, Daniel, Jack, Adam, Ella, and Lydia
S. McB.

To Di, Steve, Deirdre, and The Mice
A. J.

Text copyright © 2007 by Sam McBratney
Illustrations copyright © 2007 by Anita Jeram

Guess How Much I Love You™ is a registered trademark
of Walker Books Ltd., London.

First U.S. edition 2010

Library of Congress Cataloging-in-Publication Data is available.
Library of Congress Catalog Card Number 2009026022
ISBN 978-0-7636-4654-7

09 10 11 12 13 14 SCP 10 9 8 7 6 5 4 3 2

Printed in Humen, Dongguan, China

This book was typeset in Cochin.
The illustrations were done in
ink and watercolor.

Candlewick Press
99 Dover Street
Somerville, Massachusetts 02144

visit us at www.candlewick.com

GUESS HOW MUCH
I LOVE YOU
All Year Round

by
Sam McBratney

illustrated by
Anita Jeram

CANDLEWICK PRESS

Spring

Little Nutbrown Hare
and Big Nutbrown Hare went
hopping in the fresh spring air.

Spring is when things start
growing after winter.

They saw a tiny acorn growing.

"Someday it will be a tree,"
said Big Nutbrown Hare.

"A big, big tree?"

"Oh, a mighty tree,"
said Big Nutbrown
Hare.

Little Nutbrown Hare spotted a tadpole
in a pool. It was a tiny tadpole,
as wriggly as
could be.

"It will grow up to be a frog,"
said Big Nutbrown Hare.

"Like that frog over there?"

"Just the same as that one,"
said Big Nutbrown Hare.

A hairy caterpillar slowly crossed the path in front of them, in search of something green to eat.

"One day soon it will change into a butterfly," said Big Nutbrown Hare.

"With wings?"

"Oh, lovely wings," said
Big Nutbrown Hare.

And then they found a bird's nest
among the rushes. It was full of eggs.

"What does an egg turn into?" asked
Little Nutbrown Hare.

"A bird."

"A big, big bird?"

"Well . . . a grown-up bird,"
said Big Nutbrown Hare.

Does nothing stay the same? thought Little Nutbrown Hare. Does everything change?

Then he began to laugh.

"What does a little
brown hare like
me turn into?"
he asked.

Big Nutbrown Hare
began to think,

and think. . . .

Goodness me, did he
know the answer?

Yes, he did!

"You'll be a Big Nutbrown Hare—like me!"

Summer

Little Nutbrown Hare
and Big Nutbrown Hare were down
by the river on a summer's day.

On a bright summer's day, there
are colors everywhere.

"Which blue do you like best?"
asked Little Nutbrown Hare.

Big Nutbrown Hare didn't know—
there were so many lovely blues.

"I think . . . maybe the sky,"
he said.

Big Nutbrown Hare
looked across the river.
There were grasses and ferns
and tall plants swaying
in the breeze.

"Which green do you
like best?" he asked.

Little Nutbrown Hare began to think,
but he didn't really know.
So many lovely things
were green.

"Maybe the big leaves," he said.

Now it was
Little Nutbrown
Hare's turn to
pick a color.

He spotted a ladybug and some poppies.

"What's your favorite
red?" he asked.

Big Nutbrown Hare
thought about red things,
but it was hard to choose
just one.

"I think maybe
those berries,"
he said.

Big Nutbrown Hare nibbled
a dandelion leaf.

"Which yellow do you
like best?"

There were so many yellows!
Little Nutbrown Hare even
saw some yellows
buzzing about.
How could he
possibly choose?

"Maybe these flowers,"
he said.

Then Little Nutbrown Hare began
to smile and smile.

He looked at Big Nutbrown Hare and said,

"Which brown do you like best?"

And Big Nutbrown Hare smiled too.
There were many many lovely browns,
but one was the best of all . . .

"Nutbrown!"

Autumn

Little Nutbrown Hare
and Big Nutbrown Hare went out
in the autumn wind.

On a windy day
the leaves were blowing.

They chased after falling leaves
until Big Nutbrown Hare
could chase no more.

"I have to have a rest!" he said.

Then a big brown box came rolling
by, blown by the autumn wind.
Little Nutbrown Hare caught
up with the box when it got
stuck in a bush.

What a nice big box!
It was great for
jumping over . . .

jumping on . . .

and jumping in.

Big Nutbrown Hare was resting under a tree when a big brown box appeared in front of him. It gave one hop and then stood absolutely still.

"I'm a box monster!" shouted the box.

Goodness me!
Big Nutbrown Hare
wondered if he was
dreaming, for he had
never heard of a box
monster before.

The box, or the monster—
or maybe the box monster—
took two hops forward.

"Here I come!" roared the box,
hopping its biggest hop yet.
Big Nutbrown Hare
jumped behind the tree.

"I wonder if I should run away!" said Big Nutbrown Hare.

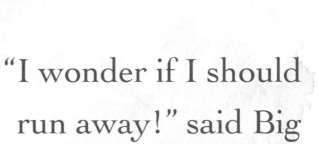

"No!" shouted the box, which suddenly flew into the air. "It's only me!"

And there was Little Nutbrown Hare, who could hardly stop laughing.

"You're not a monster,"
said Big Nutbrown Hare.

"But guess what."

"What?"

"I'm a big nutbrown monster—
and I'm coming to
get you!"

And so he did.

Winter

Little Nutbrown Hare
and Big Nutbrown Hare went
out in the winter snow.

They played I Spy as they
hopped through the snow.
Little Nutbrown Hare
looked around until he
saw something interesting.

"I spy something that belongs
to a tree," he said.

Big Nutbrown Hare
did some thinking
about trees.

"Could it be a leaf?"

That was the right answer!

Now it was Big Nutbrown
Hare's turn to look around him.

"I spy something that
belongs to a spider."

"A web!" said
Little Nutbrown Hare.

Yes! A web was the answer.

"I spy something that
belongs to a bird," said
Little Nutbrown
Hare.

Big Nutbrown
Hare thought
about birds
for a while.

Then he said, "Could it be a feather?"

Yes! It was a feather.

"This time," said
Big Nutbrown Hare, "I spy something that
belongs to the river. And it's wet, wet, wet."

"Water!" cried Little Nutbrown Hare.

Water was the answer.

Little Nutbrown Hare began to laugh.
I've got a good one, he thought.
"I spy something that belongs to me."

Big Nutbrown Hare was puzzled.
"Can I have a clue?" he said.

"It's only there when the
sun comes out."

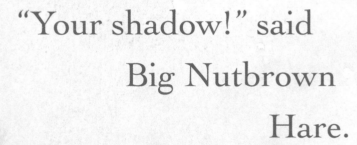

"Your shadow!" said
Big Nutbrown
Hare.

Then Big Nutbrown Hare said,
"I spy something that belongs to *me*
and it's not my shadow."

This was a really tricky one.

Little Nutbrown Hare did some
thinking, and then he said,
"Can I have a clue?"

"It's little. . . . It's nutbrown. . . .
It's my most favorite thing. . . .

And it can hop."

"It's me!"